Shirley Jackson

9 MAGIC WISHES

PICTURES BY **Miles Hyman**

Farrar Straus Giroux / New York

Text copyright © 1963, 2001 by the Shirley Jackson Estate
Illustrations copyright © 2001 by Miles Hyman
All rights reserved
Distributed in Canada by Douglas & McIntyre Ltd.
Color separations by Hong Kong Scanner Arts
Printed and bound in the United States of America by Berryville Graphics
Typography by Judy Lanfredi
First published in 1963 by the Crowell-Collier Press with illustrations by Lorraine Fox
First Farrar, Straus and Giroux edition, 2001
3 5 7 9 10 8 6 4 2

Library of Congress Cataloging-in-Publication Data
Jackson, Shirley, 1919–1965.
    9 magic wishes / Shirley Jackson ; pictures by Miles Hyman.
        p. cm.
    Summary: A child meets a magician who grants eight wonderfully fantastic
wishes, with one wish left over.
    ISBN 0-374-35525-8
    [1. Wishes—Fiction.] I. Title: Nine magic wishes. II. Hyman, Miles, ill. III. Title.

PZ7.J138 Aab 2001
[E]—dc21   00-26501

For Shirley and Stanley,
their children, grandchildren, and great-grandchildren . . .

Today was a very funny day.

The sky was green and the sun was blue and all the trees were flying balloons. A magician came walking down my street. His coat was long and black and there were stars on his hat.

"I will give you nine wishes," the magician said to me. "What do you wish for?"

So I closed my eyes and wished.

1

Wish one was for an orange pony with a purple tail. He ran as fast as the wind and his eyes were blue.

2

Wish two was for a squirrel holding a nut that opens and inside is a Christmas tree.

3

Wish three was for a round little clown with a butterfly on his nose. The clown knew tricks and songs and games and the butterfly stayed on his nose.

Wish four was for a garden of flowers all made of candy.
I ate a sugar rose and a candy cane tree.

5

Wish five was for a snowman with a black hat and eyes of coal. He was so cold that I put on my mittens before I shook his hand.

Wish six was for a tiny zoo all for me, with a tiger and a lion and a bear. They were all so small I could put them in my pocket.

7

Wish seven was for a silver ship with sails of red and it carried me in the air over the tops of the trees and the tops of the houses and everybody on the ground thought I was a bird.

8

Wish eight was for a little box and inside is another box
and inside is another box and inside is another box and
inside that is an elephant.

9

"But that is only eight wishes," the magician said to me.
"You may have one more wish."

But I had an orange pony with a purple tail and a squirrel holding a nut with a Christmas tree inside and a round little clown with a butterfly on his nose and a garden of flowers all made of candy and a cold cold snowman and a tiny zoo all my own and a silver ship with sails of red and a little box with another box inside and another box inside and another box inside and inside that an elephant.

"Thank you," I said to the magician, "but there is really nothing more to wish for."

"Then there is one wish left," the magician said to me.
"I will put it here on this rock and somebody will find it
and have a magic wish."

Then he turned himself into a leaf and the wind blew him away.

Today was a very, very funny day.